THE LEGEND OF DAVE THE VILLAGER 6

by Dave Villager

First Print Edition (December 2019)

BOOK SIX:
The Robot King

The Legend of Dave the Villager 6

CHAPTER ONE

Future Dave

"Tell me about the future," said Carl. "Do I become rich? Do I get a mansion with a heated swimming pool?"

"No," said Future Dave. "You die."

"Oh," said Carl.

"You get torn apart by robot ocelots," said Future Dave. "I can still remember your screams."

"I wish I hadn't asked," said Carl.

"Hang on a second," said Dave, standing up, "this is ridiculous. How can you be me from the future? This doesn't make any sense. How did you go back in time?"

"With this," said Future Dave, taking out a purple orb from his pocket.

"That's the teleportation ender pearl thing," said Carl. "The one we took from Robo-Steve's chest."

"My team of scientists modified it so that it could teleport me through time," said Future Dave. "But it only had enough energy for one jump. I can't go back."

"Wait, I have a team of scientists in the future?" said

Dave. "That's pretty cool."

"That's because you become the leader of the resistance," said Future Dave. "The resistance against the Robot King."

"Who's the Robot King?" asked Dave.

"You've met him before," said Future Dave. "Although when you first met him he went by a different name."

"Let me guess," said Carl. "Robo-Steve?"

"Yes," said Future Dave, sounding surprised. "How did you know?"

"Well we don't know that many robots," said Carl. "So it was pretty obvious."

Dave stood up and started to pace the room. All this time travel talk was hurting his head.

"So," said Dave, "what you're saying is that in the future, Robo-Steve changes his name and takes over the world?"

"Not in the future," said Future Dave. "It's already happening now. I wanted to arrive earlier in the past, but it would have put too much strain on the pearl. In your time —right now—the Robot King has already taken over Robotropolis. Or, as you probably know it, Villagertropolis."

"Wait," said Dave, "what about Herobrine? I thought if anyone was going to take over the world, it would be him."

"Oh he tried," said Future Dave. "There was a great war between Herobrine and the Robot King. The land was ravaged and many fell, but in the end the Robot King was victorious. In my time the world is a ruin, which is why I've come back to the past, to stop the Robot King before it's too late."

"So what can we do?" asked Dave.

"In three days time, the Robot King unleashes his robot army," said Future Dave. "They go forth from Robotropolis and march from village to town, taking over. We need to stop the invasion before it starts. We need to sneak into Robotropolis and assassinate the Robot King, before it's too late."

"Wow," said Carl, rolling his eyes, "when you say it like that you make it sound so easy."

CHAPTER TWO

Saving the Future

"Er, Sally," said Dave, "do you mind looking after Porkins for a few days? Carl and I just have an errand to run in Villagertropolis."

Future Dave had insisted that they tell as few people as possible about their mission, to stop word reaching Robo-Steve. Dave hated lying to Sally, but Future Dave was very insistent.

"Of course," said Sally, smiling. She was in the kitchen, making stew. "After what you three did for Greenleaf, it's the least I can do. Er, who's that by the way?"

Dave looked round and saw Future Dave standing in the doorway of the kitchen.

"Um, that's my uncle," said Dave. "My uncle... Dave."

"Pleased to meet you," said Sally to Future Dave. "So you're called Dave too? That must get a bit confusing."

"Sometimes," said Future Dave. "My lady, do you know where we can find horses?"

"We only have pigs in Greenleaf," said Sally, "but Little Block has horse stables. That's a village about half a day north from here. It's on the way to Villagertropolis."

"Thank you kindly," said Future Dave.

Before they left, Dave and Carl went to say goodbye to Porkins. The pigman was still fast asleep, healing up from when he'd lost his arm in the Nether.

"We'll see you soon, Porkins, I promise," said Dave. "Sally will look after you."

"Sorry again about your arm," said Carl. "But if it makes you feel any better, I've got no arms—so you still have one more than me."

Dave turned to Future Dave.

"Is he going to be alright?" Dave asked. "In the future, I mean."

"Oh yes," said Future Dave. "In the future Porkins becomes a great general in the war against the Robot King. His troops call him the One-Armed Pig."

"That's not a very nice nickname," said Carl.

"Porkins doesn't mind it," said Future Dave. "My Porkins, I mean. War makes men change, and no-one changes more than Porkins does. After the Robot King slays the last of the pigmen, the ones in Little Bacon, Porkins loses all hope. He becomes a fierce leader who shows the enemy no mercy."

Dave looked at Porkins as he slept. He couldn't

imagine Porkins, the pink-faced pigman who always saw the good in everyone, becoming such a ruthless leader.

"What am I like in the future?" Carl asked. "You know, before the ocelots and the ripping apart."

Future Dave smiled.

"You and I remain good friends," he told Carl. "You're the number one fighter in my army, taking on scores of robots at a time, all by yourself. The men call you the Iron Creep."

"Don't you mean Iron *Creeper*?" asked Carl.

"No," said Future Dave.

"Iron Creep doesn't sound very nice," muttered Carl. "It makes me sound like a creep."

"But we can change all this, right?" Dave asked. "If we stop Robo-Steve now, the future will change."

"I hope so," said Future Dave. "It's the only hope we have. In my time, twenty years from now, the world is on the brink of ruin. Only a handful of mobs still exist; most have been turned into robots."

"So how did you end up time traveling back here?" Carl asked.

"The Robot King's forces had found our base," said Future Dave. "They launched a final attack, sending a huge army against us. My scientists had been trying to make a time-travel device for years. The time pearl wasn't ready yet, but we had no choice. As the robots broke in and stormed the base, I used the time pearl to come here. Since it was unfinished, it couldn't survive the trip."

He held out the purple pearl again. Dave noticed that it was covered in cracks.

"So I'm stuck here, and I only get one chance to change the future," said Future Dave.

"Wait," said Dave rummaging in his pocket. He pulled out his own purple pearl, this one un-cracked and still glowing faintly. "I still have a working teleportation pearl. Can't you turn that into another time-travely thing?"

"I wouldn't know how," said Future Dave. "The scientists did the modifications to my pearl. I don't know exactly what they did."

"That's a shame," said Carl. "I always wanted to travel in time. I could go back to when I was six and my cousin stole my baked potato, and I could punch him in the nose."

Future Dave scowled.

"Carl, this is no time for jokes."

"I wasn't joking," said Carl.

"Come on," said Dave. "If we've only got three days, we ought to get a move on."

He put his hand on Porkins's forehead.

"See you soon," Dave said. "We'll be back before you know it."

"Unless we get killed by robots," said Carl.

"Yes," said Dave. "Thank you Carl. Unless we get killed

by robots..."

CHAPTER THREE

Cool Weapons

Dave kitted himself out in a full set of diamond armor and Carl got back inside his iron golem suit. Dave offered to make Future Dave some armor, but he refused.

"I have something better than diamond," he said, opening his leather coat to reveal dark purple armor underneath. "Obsidian. The toughest armor there is. My scientists invented it."

"That is pretty cool," said Carl.

They had just left the village and were walking across a plains biome, and in the morning light Dave finally got a proper look at his future self.

Future Dave was twenty years older than Dave, but he looked even older than that. He had a thick gray beard covering most of his face, and lots of scars on his cheeks, from the many battles he'd fought in. A black eye patch covered his right eye.

He wore a brown leather coat that was so long that it almost dragged along the floor as he walked, and underneath the coat was his obsidian armor. He had a strange-looking sword stored in a scabbard on his back, as well as a bow and a quiver full of arrows. He had a trident as well, which looked like it was made of emerald.

"Come on then, Future Dave," said Carl. "Show us some of those cool future weapons you've got."

"I'm sure you'll see them in good time," said Future Dave. "If we get caught by the Robot King's forces we'll have plenty of fighting to do."

"Come ooooon," said Carl. "If you're gonna drag us along for this stupid quest, the least you can do is show us your cool weapons."

Future Dave grinned.

"I'd almost forgotten how annoying you could be, Carl," he said. "Ok, have a look at this."

He swung the green trident from his back, holding it out in front of him with both hands.

"The Trident of Emeros," said Future Dave. "An ancient weapon created by an ancient civilization of villagers. My troops found it while they were stationed at a desert pyramid."

"Come on," said Carl, "what can it do?"

"This," said Future Dave. He aimed the trident at a tree and a blast of green energy shot out of it, exploding the tree to bits.

"Wow!" said Carl.

"That was awesome!" said Dave.

Future Dave smiled.

"It's so nice to see happy faces for once," he said. "In the future, no-one has much to smile about."

Dave could see that Future Dave was starting to get sad, so he said:

"What about that bow?"

"Ah yes!" said Future Dave. He put the trident back in the sheath on his back, then pulled out the bow. It was twice as large as any bow Dave had ever seen, and was made of obsidian. Future Dave pulled an arrow from his quiver and notched it on the bow. The arrow head began to glow blue.

"Electro arrows," said Future Dave. "They have three times the range of a normal arrow and five times the power. Plus they can fire as both normal arrows..."

He fired the glowing blue arrow. It sped forward at super speed and went *thunk*, embedding itself into a tree.

"... or explosive arrows," Future Dave continued.

He pressed a button on the side of a second arrow, and the arrow head changed from glowing blue to glowing red. He fired the arrow at the tree and *BOOM*, it blew the tree to bits.

"Ok, that is really cool," said Carl. Dave had never seen the creeper so excited.

"And finally the sword," said Future Dave. He pulled it

out from the scabbard. The sword was longer than a normal blade and needed to be held in two hands, but to Dave it just looked like a normal iron sword.

"Why did you save the boring one til last?" asked Carl.

"Sword... ACTIVATE!" said Future Dave. Suddenly the blade glowed a deep red color. It was hot too—Dave could feel the heat from where he was standing.

"Wooooow," said Carl.

"A redstone-powered inferno blade," said Future Dave. "The heat from the blade can cut through robots like butter."

"I don't suppose you brought spare weapons for us?" said Carl.

"Afraid not," grinned Future Dave.

"I wish I came from the future," said Carl miserably. "The weapons are so much cooler."

"I wish you could have seen what the scientists did to your iron suit," said Future Dave. "Over the years they kept making adjustments to it. "By the end you could destroy an obsidian block with one punch, and you had blaster cannons attached to each arm."

"Wow," said Carl.

"Anyway," said Future Dave, "that's enough showing off. Let's get to Little Block and buy some horses. This road still exists in the future—after it goes through Little Block it should bring us directly to Robotropolis."

They continued to walk across the plains biome. The sun was shining brightly, and Future Dave kept grinning and holding his face up to soak up the sun.

"In the future the air is so thick with pollution that you rarely see the sun," he told them. "The Robot King's factories are always pumping out gas into the atmosphere. Plus, the war between Herobrine and the Robot King caused so much destruction that there isn't much plant life left."

"The future sounds a bit rubbish," said Carl.

"Oh it is," said Future Dave. "But we're going to change all that."

"What will happen to you after we change the future?" Dave asked.

"Well," said Future Dave, "if we stop the Robot King, there'll be no war, so I won't end up being sent back in time, so I should just disappear from your timeline. I'll reappear in my own timeline, twenty years from now, with no memory of any of this. At least, that's what my scientists thought."

"Man," said Carl, "time travel is complicated."

"Yes," said Future Dave. "That's why it's important to keep it simple and just remember the important bits. We defeat the Robot King, the war never happens, we save the future."

"Can I ask you some questions about the future?" said

Dave. "I know that we're trying to change it, so things won't be exactly the same, but there might be some information you have that will be useful to us."

"Let me guess," said Future Dave, "you want to know how to defeat Herobrine?"

"Uh, yes," said Dave.

"Afraid I can't help you," said Future Dave. "I wasn't there when it happened. All I know is that there was a big battle outside the walls of Diamond City. The Robot King's army fought Herobrine's army, and eventually the two of them ended up fighting each other. The Robot King won, slaying Herobrine and winning the war."

Dave was disappointed. He had hoped that Future Dave might know what it would take to defeat Herobrine once and for all. From all that Dave had seen, it didn't look like Herobrine could be killed by any normal methods.

"I've got another question as well," said Dave, "but this one's a bit silly..."

"Go on," said Future Dave. "If I can help in any way, I'll be glad to. Your future is my future too, remember."

"Do I... I mean, do *you*... do we ever slay the ender dragon?"

For a moment Future Dave looked confused. And then he laughed, a big, booming laugh.

"The ender dragon!" he said. "I almost forgot! My gosh, that was why we set out on our adventure in the first place, wasn't it? That all seems so long ago now."

"So that's a no?" said Dave.

"Afraid not," said Future Dave. "Once the war with the robots broke out, I forgot all about the dragon. There were more important things to worry about."

"Oh," said Dave, "I guess that makes sense."

It seemed impossible to Dave that he could ever forget about his ender dragon quest. It was all he'd thought about for so long.

I'll never give up on my quest, he vowed to himself. *No matter what else happens, eventually I'll find my way to the ender dragon.*

"I've got a question about the future too," said Carl. "Do they still have baked potatoes? Because if they don't, I might as well give up right now."

CHAPTER FOUR

On the Road

It was early afternoon when they reached Little Block. Like
Greenleaf, it was a small villager town with just a few
wooden houses. But when they got there, Dave was
surprised to see that the villagers there recognized him.

"Dave and Carl!" said a female villager in a red gown,
who turned out to be the mayor. "It's an honor to see you
again!"

Dave soon realized that the reason the villagers knew
them was that they'd been down the pit in the Nether
when Dave and the others had defeated Herobrine's
forces. The mayor explained that she and the other
villagers had been captured by zombie pigmen the night
before they were due to join Dave's rebellion, and they had
been taken by force to the pit.

"If it weren't for you, we'd all be zombies," said the
mayor. "Is there anything we can do to repay you?"

"Er, you could lend us three horses," said Dave.

"No," said the mayor. "We won't lend you three

horses, you can *have* three horses. The best horses in our stables."

The villagers brought out the horses. Unfortunately when Carl tried to mount his horse in his iron golem suit, he was so heavy that he almost broke the horse's back, so they decided to take two horses instead, and Carl would run alongside them.

"I don't get tired when using the suit," said Carl, "so I can run as much as I want. Still, it would have been nice to ride a horse."

So they set off: Dave and Future Dave riding on horses and Carl running in his iron golem suit. They must have looked quite a sight, Dave thought to himself: a villager, a future version of the same villager and a creeper wearing the body of an iron golem.

There were mountains in the distance, but the road they were following was taking them around the edge of the mountains instead of through them, Dave was pleased to see.

They rode until the sun went down, and then Dave built a small house out of the blocks in his bag, with enough room for three beds and a pen for the horses.

"Get some sleep," said Future Dave, climbing into his own bed. "We need to leave early tomorrow, as we've only got two days left."

"We could always ride through the night?" suggested

Dave.

"No," said Future Dave. "As much as we might like to, we can't stay awake for three days straight. And besides, we're going to need all our strength to defeat the Robot King."

"How hard will he be to defeat?" Dave asked. "The last time we fought him, in the Cool Dude Battle Royale, he claimed his power levels were at one-thousand percent."

"Although then he went all weird and that pigman defeated him with a single arrow," said Carl.

"I don't know how powerful he'll be," said Future Dave. "In my time, twenty years from now, the Robot King has the power of a god. But that's because he's been updating his systems and making improvements to his body for so long. I think he'll be powerful now, but we should be able to defeat him. Especially with my advanced weapons."

"There's one more thing," said Dave. "the last time we met Robo-Steve... the Robot King... whatever you want to call him... he said he'd changed. He said the electricity had changed him and he begged us to save him."

Future Dave gave Dave a fierce stare.

"Dave, I know you mean well," he said, "but I need you to remember something important: we *must* destroy the Robot King. You have no idea how much destruction and misery his actions will cause if he's left alive. I've lost so many friends. You should have seen what those robot ocelots did to Carl. It makes me shudder to even think about it."

"Ok ok, we get the picture," said Carl, miserably. "Can you please stop talking about my horrific death?"

"Please," said Future Dave, "just remember how important this mission is. If we destroy the Robot King, his entire army will be defeated. They get their orders from him: once he's gone, the threat will be gone. And you can live out the rest of your life in peace and do whatever you want after that. You can go and find the ender dragon, just like you always dreamed."

"Ok," said Dave. "I understand."

But as he lay in bed that night his mind kept going back to Robo-Steve, and how helpless he'd looked.

"*Please,*" Robo-Steve had begged them. "*Take me with you.*"

If we'd taken him with us, maybe none of this would have happened, Dave thought. *Maybe we should have shown him mercy.*

But Dave knew better than most that it was useless to think about roads not traveled. What was done was done, and there was nothing he could do to change that.

CHAPTER FIVE

The Mountains

As soon as the sun began to rise, they set off again, following the path as it wound its way round the foot of the mountains.

They came round a corner and Future Dave suddenly thrust his hand up, signaling them to stop.

Dave and Carl came in closer.

"Robot soldiers up ahead," whispered Future Dave.

"Oh yeah," said Carl, squinting. The creeper had good eyes from living in dark caves for most of his life. "What shall we do, go and beat them up?"

"No," said Future Dave. "All the robots are connected to the Robot King. If even one of them sees us, he'll know we're here. We need to keep our approach a secret, or he'll send all his forces after us."

"How big an army does he have?" asked Dave. "He can't have that many troops. It's not that long since we last saw him."

"The Robot King has converted all the factories in the

city to build his army," said Future Dave. "By the time he launches his attack, in two days time, he'll have over ten thousand soldiers."

"Ten *thousand?*" gasped Dave. "How can we ever defeat him?"

"I told you," said Future Dave. "You cut off the head of the creeper and the body dies."

"Hey!" said Carl.

"Sorry," said Future Dave. "I meant, if you slay the Robot King, his army will power down. That's why we must keep our presence a secret from him for as long as possible."

"So how do we get to Robo-Villagertropolis, or whatever it's called?" said Carl.

Future Dave looked up.

"We'll have to go through the mountains," he said.

Future Dave pulled out a compass from his pocket.

"I have this set up to point to north," he said. "If we follow it, we'll get to Robotropolis."

"I'll take your word for that," said Carl.

They began climbing up the mountain. The going was slow, finding a way up the blocks, and they soon realized that their horses were slowing them down rather than helping them.

"We'll have to release them, unfortunately," said Future Dave.

"Will they be ok?" asked Dave.

"There'll be fine," said Future Dave. "They'll find their way back home to Little Block easily."

So they said goodbye to the horses and let them go. As Future Dave had said, the horses ran off in the direction of Little Block, back down the road.

"Those horses are the sensible ones," said Carl. "They know to escape while they still can."

As they walked up the mountain the going got slower. There was snow up on the peaks, and it was starting to get cold.

"There are some llamas over there," said Dave, spotting a herd in the distance. He'd never seen a llama before, but he'd read about them. "We could tame them and ride them."

"It would take too long," said Future Dave.

"Climbing this mountain is taking too long," said Carl. "Even with my big iron legs."

"We need to find a route through the mountain," said Future Dave. "Keep your eye out for a cave entrance."

Soon they were so high up that when Dave looked round he could see for miles below them. He could see Little Block and Greenleaf in the distance, and the ocean beyond that: the same ocean that he, Carl and Porkins had crossed after the Cool Dude Battle Royale. It seemed so long ago now.

"I can see a cave," said Carl, "it's just up ahead."

Carl was right: up ahead there was a small gap in the mountain that led into darkness.

"Does anyone have any torches?" asked Carl.

"No need," said Future Dave. He pulled out his sword and said "sword activate!" and the blade lit up with red light.

CHAPTER SIX

The Cave

They entered the cave, with Future Dave's red sword lighting their way. The walls were dull and gray, but it was warmer in here than outside on the mountainside.

"You realize that sword's going to attract every mob for miles around," said Carl.

"Let them come," said Future Dave. "They don't stand a chance against all three of us."

Dave had to admit that his future self had a point. They had futuristic weapons and an iron golem suit on their side. What could go wrong?

As they got deeper into the cave, Dave saw deposits of various ores—gold, diamond, redstone and lapis lazuli— but he knew that now wasn't the time for mining. They were in too much of a rush.

On the way back to Greenleaf I'll do some mining, he thought. His resources were running a bit low, especially after creating so many weapons and pieces of armor for the battle against the zombie pigmen. Also it would be nice to just do some resource gathering, he thought. He, Carl and Porkins had got involved in so many big adventures recently that he needed a break. *I just want to punch a few trees and dig up some ore,* he thought to himself. *Is that too much to ask?*

"BUUUUURRR!!!!"

Dave was shaken from his thoughts by the sound of a zombie. The three of them turned around to see around ten zombies stumbling slowly towards them. Once that sight would have terrified Dave, but not now. Ten zombies was nothing to him, after fighting whole armies of zombie pigmen in the Nether.

"Stay back," Dave said to the zombies. "We don't want to fight you, but if you attack us we'll have no choice."

"Stupid villager," said a zombie. "We eat you now."

"No you won't," said Future Dave. Moving his hands as quick as lightning he pulled out his bow, strung a glowing arrow, pressed the button on the side of the arrow so the glowing light changed from blue to red, then fired it. The arrow exploded in the middle of the zombies, destroying them all and leaving only bits of rotted flesh behind.

"Nice," said Carl. "Can I borrow that sometime?"

"We could have convinced them to leave," Dave said to Future Dave.

"Dave, you need to stop thinking like that," said

Future Dave. "The world is full of bad guys out to get you. You can show them mercy if you want, but they won't show you any back. It's kill or be killed."

"Or blow up or be blowed up," said Carl.

Future Dave laughed. "Carl gets it. Trust me, Dave, I was you once, remember? I know how you think. But being merciful only leads to trouble."

Dave said nothing, but he didn't feel comfortable with what his future self was saying. He didn't feel too bad about slaying zombies, but he would have at least liked to have given them a chance before slaying them all. Carl was proof that bad mobs could change their ways, just as Dave was proof that villagers could be more than just traders and farmers.

They walked onwards, past underground rivers and lakes of lava, going deeper and deeper into the caves, the ground sloping gradually downwards.

"Are we definitely going the right way?" asked Carl.

"Yes" said Future Dave, checking his compass. "We're still heading north. If we keep going, we'll eventually get to Robotropolis."

They were walking through a large cavern when suddenly they heard the clattering of bones. Coming out of the darkness was a skeleton.

"Skeletons, I hate these guys," said Carl. "Are you ok with us slaying skeletons, Dave? You're not worried about their feelings?"

"Ha ha," said Dave, rolling his eyes. "No, I have nothing against slaying skeletons."

"Good," said Future Dave. He fired a glowing blue arrow at the skeleton, hitting it right in the skull. The skeleton collapsed, and then *poof*, it was gone.

"You're not feeling too sad for the skeleton, are you Dave?" said Carl.

"No," snapped Dave. "Look, the difference with zombies is that they can talk."

"You didn't mind slaying drowned," said Carl.

"As far as I know, they don't talk," said Dave. "And even if they did, they were attacking us. I'll defend myself if I need to, but I'm not going to just slay every bad mob that I see. How would you feel if we just went around slaying every creeper we saw?"

"I... good point," said Carl.

"An enemy is an enemy," said Future Dave. "Better to strike first, in my experience. If there's even a chance that a mob is a threat, I don't hesitate to act. I don't care if it's a zombie, a creeper or even a villager."

"You've slain *villagers?*" said Dave.

"Only bad ones," said Future Dave. "In the war, some villagers and pillagers went over to the Robot King's side. When I fought them in battle, I didn't hesitate. If you're going to be a *true* hero, Dave, you have to put your doubts aside. A warrior must rid himself of doubt and turn himself into a weapon."

"Are you talking about being a warrior or being a hero?" asked Dave.

"There's no difference," said Future Dave. "If a warrior fights for what he believes in, he's a hero."

"Wait, what's that sound?" said Carl.

From all around the cavern came the sound of clattering and cracking bones.

"Sword, max brightness!" said Future Dave.

His red blade glowed even brighter, illuminating the whole cavern.

All around them were hundreds of skeletons, all holding bows. A few of the skeletons were riding skeleton horses and wearing iron helmets.

"Ok," said Future Dave, with a grin. "Now *this* is a proper fight."

CHAPTER SEVEN

Skeletons

Arrows came at them from all directions. Dave raised his shield, Carl tucked his head into his iron suit and Future Dave pulled out a small disk that lit up, creating a shield made of glowing red light. The three of them stood back to back, to block the storm of arrows.

"What are we going to do?" said Dave.

"Fight," said Future Dave. He threw his glowing shield; it span through the air, slicing through a group of the skeletons, cutting them in two before burying itself in the wall of the cave.

And so the battle began. Future Dave pulled out his trident and started firing blasts of green energy at the skeletons, each green explosion sending bits of broken bone scattering across the cavern; Carl charged into the skeletons, sending them flying, then started swinging at them with his iron arms, all while keeping his head safely tucked away to avoid the arrows; and Dave charged into the skeletons with his shield raised, shield in one hand and diamond sword in the other, swinging the blade at all the skeletons he could hit.

It was a new experience for Dave, fighting foes who could fire projectile weapons. He had to make sure that he was facing the skeletons at all times, never showing them his back. It was difficult though, as the skeletons were all round the room, firing at them from every angle.

Suddenly something struck Dave, plunging into his shoulder.

"Arrrgh!!!" he yelled. He almost fell to the floor, but somehow managed to stay on his feet.

If I fall over I'll be done for, he thought. *The skeletons will fill me full of so many arrows that I'll look like a pin cushion.*

So even though he had an arrow sticking out of his shoulder, Dave fought on. Every time he swung his sword a jolt of pain ran down his arm, but he kept going; pushing through the pain and continuing to fight.

There seemed to be an endless supply of skeletons, more and more of them appearing for every one that was slain, but eventually their numbers started thinning out. Future Dave finished the last of them off with a blast from his trident, blowing the skeletons to bits.

"Wow," said Carl. "Those bony idiots don't know when to give up."

"You both fought well," said Future Dave. "But we

must keep moving."

"Can one of you help?" Dave asked. "I think I've got an arrow in my back."

"Ouch," said Carl. "That looks painful. You probably shouldn't pull it straight out."

Future Dave reached into his coat pocket, then handed Dave a bottle of red liquid.

"Potion of healing," he said. "Drink it all."

Dave took a swig from the bottle. It tasted disgusting.

"Keep drinking," said Future Dave.

Dave did as he was told. At first it felt like nothing was happening, but then his shoulder began to tingle. He looked round and saw the arrow being pushed out of his skin. Eventually it came out, landing on the floor. He ran his hand over the wound, but it had completely healed.

"Wow," said Dave. "Is that a potion from the future?"

"No," said Future Dave, "it's a pretty standard potion. You just know nothing about brewing. I should know—I used to be you."

Dave made a mental note to learn about brewing as soon as he could.

"Wait," said Carl, "did you both see that?"

"See what?" said Dave. Carl was looking down a passageway that looked, to Dave, like it was full of nothing but darkness.

"It was a creeper," said Carl. "It looked at us, then

scampered off."

"Well if it's a creeper, can't you just ask it to leave us alone?" said Dave.

"You don't understand," said Carl. "It was a *blue* creeper."

Future Dave's face went pale.

"Oh no," he said.

"I don't understand," said Dave. "Are blue creepers different to green creepers?"

"Blue and green creepers are about as different as zombie villagers and villagers," said Carl. "Blue creepers are vicious animals. They can't talk, they move twice as fast as normal creepers and their explosions are much bigger."

"Plus, they hunt in packs," said Future Dave. "Keep your weapons ready, boys. You're going to need them."

CHAPTER EIGHT

Sneaking Through the Caves

Future Dave had decided that using his sword to light the way was too dangerous from now on.

"We don't want to advertise our presence to the blue creepers," he told them. "So from now on we'll have to trust in Carl's eyesight."

What that meant, Dave soon found out, was that they were going to be walking through the pitch black cave with no light. Since Carl could see in the dark he was at the front, leading them, but Dave and Future Dave could see nothing at all.

"Are you sure this is a good idea?" Dave whispered, as he stumbled through the darkness, his arms stretched out ahead of him to stop him bumping into anything.

"It's the only choice we have," Future Dave whispered back. "Trust me, we don't want to have to deal with blue creepers."

The blue creepers must be pretty dangerous if Future Dave didn't want to deal with them, Dave thought. Future

Dave was one of the most powerful warriors Dave had ever seen, maybe up there with Steve, so if he was scared of something, it must be pretty scary.

"Where are you Carl?" Dave whispered. "Am I going the right way?"

"I'm here," said Carl. "Come on."

Dave had always hated the dark as a child, so this was all his worst fears come to life: wandering through a pitch black cave where monsters could jump out at him at any moment. He knew that Carl's eyes would see any mobs before they attacked, but Carl was only one creeper: he could only look one way at a time. What if a monster sneaked up on them from behind?

Suddenly Dave heard something: a deep, rumbling sound echoing around the walls of the cave. His blood went cold.

"W-what was that?" he said.

"Oh sorry," said Carl, "that was my belly. I'm dying for a baked potato."

To Dave's relief, the cave eventually began to get brighter.

"It must be daylight up ahead," he whispered.

"I don't think so," said Future Steve.

Future Steve was right. As they walked nearer to the light, Dave could see that it was coming from lava. They found themselves in a cavern with a lava lake in the middle. It reminded Dave of the cavern where he'd first met Porkins, and that made him sad.

I hope you're ok, Porkins, he thought to himself.

They stuck to the walls of the cavern, making their way carefully round the edge of the lake. There wasn't much room so they had to walk in single file. The lava was so close that Dave was sweating.

Dave prayed that none of the blue creepers turned up now. With lava on one side of them and the solid stone walls of the cavern on the other, they'd have nowhere to run to.

Thankfully, no blue creepers did turn up. They made it past the lava lake in one piece, without a mob in sight.

Future Dave checked his compass.

"We're still heading north," he said, "so it can't be much longer. I wish we knew how much time had passed, though. I've no idea if it's day or night."

"Then let's keep moving," said Dave. "We can't afford to risk losing any more time."

"Run!" Carl yelled.

Dave turned around just in time to see two blue creepers rushing towards them.

"Oh dear," he thought.

And then the creepers exploded.

CHAPTER NINE

Creepers!

Somehow, Dave was still alive.

He opened his eyes and saw that he, Carl and Future Dave were all inside a dome of red light. The exploding creepers had created a huge crater, but the explosions hadn't got through the red light force field.

"My holo-shield," said Future Dave. Dave noticed that he was holding the small disk that earlier had turned into the red shield. "It's strong, but I don't think it can take another hit like that."

"*HISSSSSSS!!!!*"

Dave turned to see three more blue creepers running towards them.

Future Dave turned off the force field then, moving quicker than Dave would have thought possible, he took his bow from his quiver and fired a glowing blue arrow at one of the creepers.

KABOOM!!!!!

The creeper exploded in a blast of blue light, the

explosion taking the other two creepers out as well.

Dave, Carl and Future Dave were alive, but the cavern was full of huge craters. The banks of the lava lake had been broken, and the lava was flowing across the room.

"More blue creepers!" Carl yelled.

He was right. Blue creepers were rushing at them from every side, hissing loudly. They seemed to care nothing for their own lives, some of them falling into the lava lake and exploding.

Dave took out his wooden bow, and he and Future Dave fired arrow after arrow at the creepers, each one exploding in a blast of blue light and tearing the cavern to shreds.

The tiny piece of ground they were standing on was almost surrounded by lava now, with nowhere to run to.

"This is just typical," said Carl. "Just when I start to think I could maybe become a hero, reality comes along and slaps me in the face."

"Well," said Dave, firing another arrow at a blue creeper. "At least it can't get any worse."

Suddenly they heard a terrible shriek from somewhere deep inside the caves.

"Oh no," said Carl.

"What is it?" said Dave.

"That's a queen," said Carl. "A blue creeper queen."

The cavern began to shake. *DOOM! DOOM! DOOM!*

DOOM!

"Is that an earthquake?" said Dave.

"No," said Future Dave. "Those are footsteps."

The blue creepers continued to run at them, and Dave and Future Dave continued to shoot arrows at them, but behind the explosions Dave could hear the huge footsteps getting closer and closer.

"This isn't good," said Carl. "Not good at all!"

"Have you ever fought a blue creeper queen before?" Dave asked Future Dave.

"No," said Future Dave. "A squadron of my men ran into one once though."

"What happened to them?" asked Dave.

"Nothing good," said Future Dave. "Let's just say, when they left the base they were a squadron of two-hundred, and when they came back home they were a squadron of two."

"What are we going to do?" whimpered Carl.

"We'll fight to the end," said Future Dave. "I'm not afraid to die in battle."

"Well I am," said Carl. "I always wanted to die doing what I loved best—eating baked potatoes and complaining about things."

This can't be how it ends, Dave thought desperately. Future Dave had fought so many battles for so many years that it seemed that he didn't know how to do anything but fight, and Carl was panicking so much that he wasn't going to be of any help.

Then it's up to me, thought Dave. *I have to get us out of this mess.*

He took a look at their surroundings, taking it all in. They were in a room full of lava, with blue creepers rushing at them from every angle, and some sort of huge creeper queen on the way. It didn't look good.

If they tried to escape into one of the tunnels that led out of the cavern, they'd either get blown to bits by the blue creepers, or they might bump into the creeper queen. If they dug down, they'd end up deeper inside the mountain, and might end up bumping into more blue creepers or falling into more lava. So, Dave reasoned, the only thing they could do was go up.

"Here," he said, reaching into his bag and handing Carl and Future Dave a handful of tiny blocks. "We need to go up."

"Go up?" said Future Dave. "What are you talking about? We need to fight!"

"No," said Dave. "We need to escape. Come on."

Dave jumped in the air, quickly placing a dirt block under his feet. Then he jumped in the air again, placing a wood block on top of the dirt one. Then he jumped in the air a third time, placing a cobblestone block on top of the wood one.

Dave looked down at Future Dave and Carl.

"Come on," he said. "Let's get out of here!"

Future Dave and Carl looked at each other, then started quickly building towers of their own. The three of them built their towers up and up, getting nearer and nearer to the roof of the cavern.

Below them the blue creepers rushed at the towers, exploding into them, but Dave, Carl and Future Dave were so high up now that the explosions couldn't reach them.

The three of them finally reached the roof of the ceiling.

"Do you two have pickaxes?" Dave asked them.

"No," said Carl. "I've only recently had arms, so this is all new to me."

Dave threw Carl a spare diamond pickaxe he had in his bag, and Carl caught it in his iron hand.

"I suppose you have some sort of super obsidian pickaxe?" Dave said to Future Dave.

"Actually," Future Dave grinned, "it's diamond. But it is a redstone-powered, automatic one."

He pulled out a diamond pickaxe, pressed a button on the side and the head of the pickaxe began to vibrate.

"Show off," smiled Dave.

The three of them were just about to start digging through the ceiling when *KRADOOOOOM*—one of the walls of the cavern blasted open below them, and a huge blue creature crawled out.

Dave looked down in horror as the biggest creeper he'd ever seen crawled across the cavern, its huge, tree-trunk sized legs splashing through the lava. As well as being much, much bigger than a normal blue creeper, it had four long legs that allowed it to move around like a crab, scuttling from side to side.

The creeper queen raised its head, looking up at Dave and the others, then it let out a terrible scream.

"EIYYEEEEEE!!!!"

It opened its mouth and a blast of blue fire blasted out. Future Dave quickly raised his shield, creating another red light barrier around them, but it kept flickering, the shield unable to to take the strain.

"Keep digging up!" Future Dave yelled. "I'll hold it off as long as I can!"

"What about you?" said Dave.

"If you defeat the Robot King, it won't matter about me," said Future Dave. "My past will change and I won't even be here. So go!"

Dave and Carl began digging upwards. Every time they broke a block above them they would jump up, placing another block underneath their feet. Carl's iron body was so big that he had to break two blocks above him each time.

Dave jumped up, placed another block underneath his

feet and suddenly he was in complete darkness. The block below him had sealed him away from the cavern, so he couldn't see what was going on down there anymore. He could hear the faint sounds of the creeper queen screaming, but that was about it.

Don't worry Future Dave, Dave thought to himself. *We'll change the future, just like you wanted.*

Dave kept digging straight up, but then he began to get worried that he might dig up into another lava lake and would end up with lava pouring down on his head, so he started digging diagonally instead, his logic being that if lava started pouring down the slope towards him, he'd have time to put down a block and stop it.

Dave dug and dug until, finally, he broke a block and saw daylight shining down on him. It was so bright that he had to shield his eyes.

He climbed out of the tunnel and saw he was on the side of the mountain. Far below him a huge city stretched out into the distance. It was so big that it made Cool City look like a village.

"Wow," he said.

"Pretty impressive, huh?"

It was Carl. He was sitting on the side of the mountain in his iron golem suit.

"Carl, I'm so glad you're ok," said Dave happily.

"You know me, my life is nothing but a series of happy

events," said Carl. "It's a shame about Future Dave though."

"Yeah," said Dave.

"I hope he gave that creeper queen a good fight," said Carl.

"I'm sure he did," said Dave. "I'm sure he did."

The sun was starting to go down, Dave noticed.

"Come on," he said to Carl, "let's build a shelter and get some sleep. We've got one day left. One day to stop Robo-Steve before he starts his war."

CHAPTER TEN

Bad Dreams

Porkins was dreaming of mushroom stew.

In his dream he was swimming in a huge lake of stew, drinking as much of it as he liked. His family were there and all of his old pigman friends.

"You know, sir," Porkins said to his father. "I had a terrible dream that you were all turned into zombies. Can you believe that? What a laugh!"

"That was no dream, dear boy," his father replied. Then Porkins noticed, to his horror, that his father's face had become green and rotten, the gray skull showing underneath. He turned round and all the other pigmen were rotting away too.

"Why didn't you save us, Porkins?" they were saying, as they started swimming after him. "Why did you let this happen to us?"

Porkins tried to swim away, but one of his arms was missing, and he kept going round in circles.

"Help!" he yelled, as he began to sink into the stew,

"someone help me!"

Porkins sat up in bed in a dark room, his whole body dripping with sweat.

"What a nightmare," he gasped.

The door opened and Sally ran in, holding a torch.

"Porkins, you're awake!" she said. "Are you ok? I heard screaming."

"I... I had a horrible dream," he said. "I dreamed I lost my arm."

"Um, that wasn't a dream," said Sally nervously. "I'm sorry Porkins, but... you did lose an arm."

Porkins looked down and saw that she was telling the truth: his right arm was gone, cut off at the shoulder.

"Oh gosh," he said sadly.

"I'll go and make you some stew," said Sally.

"No!" said Porkins. "Sorry... just anything but stew. Please."

After Sally had left the room, Porkins sat on the side of the bed, looking at the space where his arm had used to be. It all came back to him: the battle with the zombie pigman; a drop of the zombie potion landing on his arm; Dave cutting off his arm to stop him turning fully into a zombie.

The skin where his arm had been had healed up so perfectly that it almost looked like he'd never had an arm at all. *Sally must have used a healing potion,* Porkins thought. Back in the Nether, before Herobrine, Porkins's tribe had been great users of potion. Porkins couldn't brew much himself, but his mother had been a master potion maker. In the harsh world of the Nether, with ghasts and lava at every turn, there was always a need for more healing potion.

Sally came back in with some pumpkin pie. Porker eagerly wolfed it down.

"How long has it been since the battle?" he asked Sally, his mouth full of pie.

"Two days," said Sally. "Most of the Greenleaf villagers are in the Nether now, helping to dismantle Herobrine's iron structures."

"Are the nether portals still active?" Porkins asked. He was thinking of the portal to Little Bacon.

"For now," said Sally. "Some of the villagers from other settlements are helping to dismantle Herobrine's buildings, so it helps if they all have an easy way to get to the Nether. But the plan is to eventually shut down the portals as well. It's just too easy for Herobrine, or another villain like him, to take over again if the portals are left standing."

"Then I must go," said Porkins. "I can't risk getting cut off from my fellow pigman. The only way I know how to get to Little Bacon is through the portals. Once the iron corridors are destroyed I'll have no way of knowing how to get there."

"You need rest," said Sally. "Why not wait until Dave and Carl get back?"

"Wait," said Porkins, "where are Dave and Carl?"

CHAPTER ELEVEN

The Neuro-Helmet

Dave and Carl were nearing the walls of Villagertropolis. They'd woken up at a first light, making their way down the mountain as quickly as they could, and now they were making their way through the fields and farms that surrounded the city.

There were huge fields of wheat and other crops, as well as fields of sheep, cows and pigs, all separated from each other by fences.

They were walking through a field of cows when Dave spotted something in the distance.

"Look," he whispered to Carl, "there's a farmhouse over there. And a farmer. We can ask him about the situation inside the city. He might even know a way we can sneak inside."

So they walked over to the farmhouse. The farmer was loading crates of carrots into a cart attached to the back of a horse, but there was something wrong, Dave thought.

"What's that stupid thing on his head?" Carl

whispered.

The farmer was wearing an iron helmet, but there were two metal poles sticking out the top of it. On top of the metal poles were two red light bulbs that kept flashing.

There was something off about the farmer as well. As he packed the carrots into the cart, his face was completely expressionless, his eyes staring blankly into the distance.

"He looks like a weirdo," whispered Carl. "Let's keep going."

"Maybe that's how they dress in Villagertropolis," Dave whispered back. "That helmet could be a fashion item."

"Fashion is for losers," said Carl. "That's why creepers prefer to go around naked. Because we're cool."

Dave stepped forward.

"Hello there," he said to the villager. "A lovely day we're having, isn't it?"

The villager stopped packing the crates, and turned his head to look at Dave.

"Light levels are satisfactory for crop growth," said the villager, in a bored voice. "If rain levels continue to be as frequent as they have been in recent months, the harvest will continue to yield sufficient food to feed the population."

"Riiiight," said Dave.

Carl sidled up next to Dave.

"I think he might be a robot," Carl whispered,

"Negative," said the farmer. "My mob ID is villager."

"Then why are you speaking in that dumb way?" asked Carl.

"My cognitive functions are being improved by my neuro-helmet," The farmer said, pointing to his iron helmet. "It allows me to think logically, bypassing emotions and allowing me to live a more efficient life. Since wearing the helmet I have become fifty-three percent more efficient at farming."

"Did you put that helmet on of your own choice?" said Dave. "Or was that Robo-Steve's doing?"

"If by Robo-Steve you are referring to the Robot King, then yes," said the villager. "The Robot King's soldiers forced me to wear the neuro-helmet, but since wearing it I have become more efficient and I no longer worry or feel sad, so these are all positives improvements."

"So this is how Robo-Steve takes over the world," said Dave to Carl. "He forced everyone to wear these helmets so he can control their brain."

"Negative," said the farmer. "My brain is not under direct control by the Robot King. The neuro-helmet simply allows me to think in a perfectly logical way. And using logic I have determined that the Robot King is the only leader who can make this world run at one-hundred percent efficiency."

"Ok, I've heard enough," said Carl, stepping forward in his iron golem suit. "Let's get that stupid thing off of his head."

"Wait," said Dave. "What if removing it scrambles his brain?"

"Come on," said Carl, "you've heard the way he talks. How much more scrambled can his brain get?"

Carl reached down and began to pull off the helmet. It was stuck onto the farmer's head tightly, but the farmer just stood there and let Carl try and remove it.

"What are you doing?" the farmer asked Carl in a bored voice. "Are you attempting to remove my neuro-helmet?"

Then *POP*, the helmet came off.

Suddenly the farmer's face began to change. His bored expression was gone, replaced by a look of horror.

"Oh thank goodness!" he said, running forward and hugging Carl's iron leg. Tears were running down his face. "Thank you, thank you, thank you!"

"Get off," said Carl. "I think I preferred you when you were all robotic."

"Can you tell us what happened?" Dave said to the farmer. "Can you tell us how Robo-Steve took over your city?"

"The Robot King, you mean?" said the farmer, wiping the tears from his eyes. "Aye, I will. But first I need a drink."

CHAPTER TWELVE

Tom the Farmer

The farmer poured Dave and Carl both a cup of warm milk.

"I'm Tom, by the way," said the farmer, sitting down opposite them at the table in the kitchen.

"Dave," said Dave.

"Carl," said Carl.

"Can you tell us about Robo-Steve's invasion?" asked Dave.

"Well, at first it was no invasion," said Tom. "The Robot King saved us. We'd been attacked by those undead pig people things. One day one of those purple portals appeared outside of our wall, and all the pig people poured out. They attacked our wall, and we attacked them back. We're only villagers, so we didn't know much about fighting, but some of our blacksmiths had built weapons for Steve before, so they knew how to make swords and armor.

"We fought back against the pigs as best we could, but

we were losing terribly. Then, from nowhere, an army of robots appeared. The all looked like robot Steves, with glowing red eyes. They defeated the pigs and saved the day.

"The trouble started later, when the leader of the robots, the Robot King, declared that he was in charge of the city now, and commanded everyone to wear one of his electronic helmet thingies. Anyone who refused was captured, and a helmet forced onto their head.

"I tried to run, but the robots caught me. They put the helmet on my head, and suddenly I didn't feel like running anymore. All my emotion—my anger at the robots, my love for my farm—it all disappeared. All I could think about was logic. I suddenly knew the most logical way to grow my crops, what to do to make sure my chickens produced the most eggs, all that stuff. Everyone else in the city is the same. They're all still working, but doing their jobs in the most logical way, without emotion."

"Like robots," said Carl.

"Aye, like robots," agreed Tom.

"It's too complicated to explain, but we need to get inside the city today," said Dave. "The Robot King is going to launch his invasion this afternoon. He's planning on taking over the whole world."

"Basically, do you know a secret way into Villagertropolis?" said Carl.

"Could we just dig underneath the wall and dig our way up when we're underneath the city?" said Dave.

"I'm afraid not," said Tom. "From what I hear, the Robot King has sensors underneath the whole city. If you try and dig through them you'll set off an alarm, and every robot in the place will be after you."

"There must be another way," said Dave.

"There is," said Tom. "But it's not pretty."

"Don't worry," said Carl. "Neither is Dave."

"In fact," said Tom, "it's downright ugly."

"So is Dave," said Carl.

"Ok," said Tom, "I'll show you."

CHAPTER THIRTEEN

Brown Water

Tom brought them to a nearby river. At first Dave couldn't figure out why, as the river wasn't flowing anywhere near the city, let alone through it, but then he save an iron pipe sticking out of the side of the river, pumping brown sludge into it.

"Oh no," said Carl, "that's not what I think it is, is it?"

"It's the sewer," said Tom, with a grin. "It pumps all the waste from the city into the river. The river then carries it all the way to the sea."

"Why's the sewer water brown?" Carl asked, looking horrified.

"Sometimes it's best not to ask too many questions," said Tom.

So Dave and Carl went over to the sewer pipe. The entrance was covered in iron bars. They would be easy to break with an iron pickaxe, but to get the right angle, they'd have to get in the water, Dave realized.

"You go first," said Carl. "I'll stay with Tom and keep

him company."

The water stank like crazy, but Dave knew they couldn't afford to waste any more time. He lowered himself gently into the river, making sure to keep his head above the water, then swam over to the pipe. The water coming out of the pipe was thick and disgusting, and it was all he could do not to throw up, but somehow Dave managed to hack away at the iron bars with his pickaxe and break them.

"Right," he called up at Carl, who was watching him from the riverbank. "You're gonna have to get in too now."

"Can't I just stay here with Tom?" said Carl. "I think I'd make a good farmer. I can milk the sheep, sheer the cows..."

"Carl!" said Dave.

"Ok, ok," moaned Carl. He lowered himself slowly into the river.

"Wait," said Tom, "will you be able to swim in that there iron suit?"

"Oh," said Carl, "I never thought of that."

Suddenly Carl lost his grip on the side of the riverbank, and went *SPLOOSH* into the water.

"Help!" he yelled, "I'm sinking!"

Carl disappeared below the water.

"Carl!" yelled Dave.

Suddenly Carl burst up from the water, grabbing onto

the bottom of the sewer pipe.

"Bluurrrghh!!!" he spluttered. "It went in my mouth."

"Well, at least we've learned that iron golems can't float," said Dave, laughing.

"I wish you'd learn to shut up," said Carl.

Carl clambered into the sewer pipe, then pulled Dave up after him.

"Thank you for all your help," Dave said to Tom, who was watching them from the river bank.

"Yes, thank you for guiding us to this disgusting sewer," said Carl.

"Good luck, you two," said Tom. "Make sure to give that Robot King what for!"

"We will," promised Dave.

"Only... don't be too harsh on him."

Dave was surprised.

"How come?" he asked Tom.

"Well, the Robot King is bad, don't get me wrong," said Tom, "but he did defeat the pigmen. And he didn't actually slay anyone when he took over."

"He took over without killing anyone?" said Dave, amazed.

"I think so," said Tom. "Although taking over a city and putting all of its citizens under mind control is still pretty bad, I suppose."

"Well... we'll see what we can do," said Dave.

"Goodbye Tom."

Dave and Carl began walking through the sewer. The smell was so bad that it made Dave's eyes water.

At first they had to wade through the disgusting brown water, but after a while the tunnel got wider and there was a walkway along the side, much to Dave and Carl's relief.

"You know, no matter what that farmer says, we need to destroy the Robot King," said Carl. "You heard what Future Dave said; All those terrible things that will happen if the Robot King takes over. I'll be honest with you, I don't really want to be torn apart by robot ocelots."

"I know," said Dave. "Don't worry. When the time comes, I'll do what I have to do."

CHAPTER FOURTEEN

The One-Armed Pig

"Where are you going?" Sally said, running after Porkins. He was walking down the road that led away from Greenleaf village, his rucksack slung over his shoulder.

"I need to make sure the chaps are ok," said Porkins. "If they're going to Villagertropolis they could be in danger. When I was in the Nether, spying on the witches in their cobblestone castle, I overheard that a robot army had taken over the city."

"Porkins," said Sally, "you've only got one arm!"

"I only need the one to hold a sword," said Porkins, with a grin.

"Ok," she said, "but I'm coming with you."

So Sally and Porkins set off for Little Block, planning to buy some horses to help them get to Villagertropolis.

"Are you sad about your arm?" Sally asked.

"I... I am a bit," said Porkins. "Mostly I'm sad that I'll never be able to fire a bow and arrow again. I was always better with a bow than I was with a sword, so I'm going to have to practice my sword technique."

"So you're still going to travel with Dave and Carl, doing hero stuff?" asked Sally.

"I don't know," said Porkins sadly. "I promised Dave that I'd stay with him to the end, to slay the ender dragon alongside him, but now that I know that there are more pigmen in the world, I don't know what to do. Should I join the chaps at Little Bacon, or stay with Dave and Carl?

"Anyway," he said, "I've been blabbing away about myself this whole time. How are you feeling? About Adam and all that?"

Sally sighed.

"If Adam came back now I wouldn't know whether to hug him or punch him in the face," she said. "I know he was only doing what he thought was best for me and him, but he betrayed the village. People were slain because of him. I don't think I can ever forgive him."

"Where do you think he went?" asked Porkins.

"I've no idea," said Sally. "He doesn't have any family elsewhere. I don't think he's even left the village before. I just hope he's ok, wherever he is."

"I'm sure he is," said Porkins. He didn't know what else to say.

CHAPTER FIFTEEN

Villagertropolis

"Look," said Dave. "There's a ladder up ahead."

"Thank goodness," said Carl. "I don't think I can stand being in this disgusting sewer a moment longer."

They'd been walking through the sewer for what seemed like hours. It was pitch black, so Dave had kept laying down torches, exhausting his coal supply.

Dave climbed up the ladder, Carl following behind him. The ladder led up a narrow vertical tunnel, and Dave could see a tiny square of daylight at the top.

"It's not easy climbing a ladder in an iron golem suit," Carl complained. "I can barely fit through this tunnel."

"Well it would be even harder if you weren't wearing it," said Dave. "You don't have any arms, remember."

"Oh yeah," said Carl.

They kept climbing, up and up and up, until Dave reached an iron trapdoor, with daylight shining down through it. He gave it a push, but it wouldn't budge.

"What's wrong?" Carl asked. "Why have you stopped?"

"This trap door... I can't get it to open," said Dave.

"Is there a switch nearby?" said Carl.

Dave felt around in the shadows. The walls of the tunnel were disgusting and slimy, and it made Dave feel sick to touch them, but eventually he found what he was looking for: a rectangular switch. He pressed it and the trapdoor swung open.

Dave peered out of the top of the trapdoor and saw that they were in the middle of a street, surrounded by huge iron skyscrapers. The buildings were huge: even taller than the ones in Cool City had been.

"I think the coast is clear," Dave whispered to Carl. It looked like there was no-one about.

The two of them clambered out of the trapdoor, then they stood in awe, looking up at the huge buildings.

"Where is everyone?" said Carl.

The streets were completely empty. And so *clean* as well. There was no rubbish, and all the buildings were spotless, their iron surfaces glistening in the sun.

But then Dave noticed that there *were* villagers walking around, but they were walking so silently that he hadn't even noticed them.

A villager in an apron was standing next to a food cart full of cooked chicken. Another villager came up to him, handed him a couple of emeralds and took a chicken—all without saying a word.

"They're all wearing those stupid helmets," said Carl.

He was right, Dave saw. Each villager was wearing a neuro helmet, the red lights on the top flashing occasionally.

It was really eerie, Dave thought, seeing so many people but hearing so little sound. He and Carl went up to one of the windows of a building and looked inside. It seemed to be a department store: store clerks were serving and customers were buying, but no-one was saying anything.

"Let's go and ask someone the way to Robo-Steve," said Carl. "Maybe he's got a palace or something."

"We're meant to be sneaking in," Dave reminded him.

"You heard what Tom the farmer said," said Carl. "The villagers aren't spying for Robo-Steve or connected to his mind, the helmets are just suppressing their emotions, making them all weird and logical. It's the robots we've got to watch out for, and I can't see any around here."

"Ok," said Dave. "Let's try it."

They walked up to the villager in the apron. He looked at them blankly.

"Um, hello," said Dave.

"Hello," said the villager.

"Do you know which way we should go to get to the Robot King?" said Dave.

"Yes," said the villager.

"Well, can you tell us?" said Carl, sounding annoyed.

"I can tell you," said the villager.

"Well?!" said Carl.

"Well what?" replied the villager.

"I think I'm going to explode," muttered Carl. "Faulty fuse or not."

"Um... please tell us how to get to the Robot King," said Dave.

"Certainly," said the villager. "Go two blocks north, three blocks west and you will reach Hero's Square. There is a high probability that the Robot King will be there, as he is preparing his army for war."

"Thanks," said Dave.

"You're welcome," said the villager.

"Come on," Dave said to Carl, "it sounds like we've got no time to lose."

"Ok," said Carl, grinning, "there's something I've been waiting to try."

CHAPTER SIXTEEN

Robots!

CLANG! CLANG! CLANG!

Carl's heavy iron feet clanged across the cobblestone as he ran along the street, Dave riding on his shoulders.

"Are you sure this is a good idea?" said Dave. "I feel like I'm going to fall off!"

"You'll be fine," said Carl, "I can run faster than you, so this is the easiest way."

Carl was right, Dave had to admit. In his iron golem suit he could run as fast as a horse, and they were making speedy progress across the city. Dave was constantly amazed at the buildings in Villagertropolis: there were lots of huge skyscrapers, but also older-looking buildings made of brick and stone. There were parks and gardens and so many beautiful places, but it was still so *quiet*. All the villagers walking back and forth barely said a word to each other, all of them staring blankly as they went about their day-to-day business.

"We're nearly there I think," said Carl. "He said three

blocks west, didn't he?"

"I think so," said Dave.

Then Dave saw something up ahead that made his heart jump.

"Stop!" he whispered to Carl.

Carl came to a stop.

"What is it?" he asked.

"Look, up ahead," said Dave. Ahead of them, on a street corner, was one of the midnight-blue robots they'd seen on the road. Even from a distance they could see its eyes glowing red.

"So what?" said Carl. "It's one robot. Let's go smash it."

"No," said Dave, "remember what future me said—the robots are all connected to Robo-Steve. If one of them sees us, he'll know we're here."

Just then, the Robot turned its head and looked right at them. Its red eyes began to flash rapidly and it opened its mouth wide, the sound of a siren coming out of it.

"I think it's spotted us," said Dave.

"Really?" said Carl. "How can you tell?"

The robot started running towards them, its feet moving so quickly that they were a blur.

Suddenly other robots appeared too, coming out from alleyways and around street corners, all running at super speed. They all surrounded Dave and Carl, their eyes flashing. They all looked like robot versions of Steve, but made of shiny blue metal.

"INTRUDERS!" said the robot who'd first spotted them. "COME WITH US FOR NEURO-HELMET FITTING."

"I think we'll pass," said Carl. "Wearing a helmet would mess up my hair."

"ERROR DETECTED," said a robot. "YOU HAVE NO HAIR."

"Oh yeah," said Carl. "You're right."

And then WHAM, he slammed his huge iron arm into the robots, sending a group of them flying.

Dave jumped off of Carl's shoulders, pulling out his diamond sword. The robots ran at them and he slashed at them, cutting two of them in half.

The robots kept coming, and Dave and Carl kept fighting them off, Dave swinging at them with his sword and Carl with his iron golem arms. But for every robot they destroyed, more came to replace them. Dave could see hordes or robots appearing from every street and side street, all of them rushing towards him and Carl.

"There's too many of them," said Dave.

"Thank you, Captain Obvious," said Carl. "I can see that."

Dave tried to swing his sword hand but a robot grabbed his arm. Other robots were grabbing his legs, stopping him from moving. He could see Carl struggling as well, robots clinging onto his iron limbs, weighing him down.

Dave fell to the ground, dropping his diamond sword, lots of robot hands pinning him down.

"INTRUDERS CAPTURED," said one of the robots.

CHAPTER SEVENTEEN

Captured

Dave and Carl were marched through the city, surrounded by an army of blue robots.

"Where are you taking us?" he kept asking, even though he had already guessed the answer.

They're taking us to Robo-Steve, he thought miserably. He and Carl had let Future Dave down.

"Stupid robots," muttered Carl, as one of the robots gave him a push. "I'm going as fast as I can."

The robots had removed Carl from his iron golem suit, so now he was just a creeper again, with tiny legs. As far as Dave knew, they'd just left the suit behind in the street.

They came round a corner and in front of them was a huge plaza, surrounded by old buildings. In the middle of the plaza was a statue of Steve made of prismarine. It looked very old.

"Great, that's all I need," said Dave. "To be reminded of Steve. I bet he never gets captured like this."

"Probably not," said Carl. "We could sure do with his

help right now, though."

They were marched across the plaza, to a huge building on the other side. It was made of polished granite, with a prismarine dome on the top. It looked like some sort of palace or government building, and Dave guessed that it must be where Robo-Steve was ruling from.

The robots brought them through the grand front entrance of the building, and they found themselves in a huge lobby with plush carpets and walls made of dark wooden planks. They were marched up some stairs, then some more stairs, until they found themselves in a grand room with a high ceiling and paintings all over the walls.

On a prismarine throne sat a golden Steve robot. He was wearing a diamond crown and had glowing purple eyes.

"Come on then, golden boy," Carl said to the robot. "Let's get this over with. Take us to your leader. Take us to Robo-Steve."

The gold robot stood up.

"I am Robo-Steve," he said. "Or at least I was—I call myself the *Robot King* now. Welcome villager, welcome creeper, I have been looking forward to seeing you again."

CHAPTER EIGHTEEN

How to Build a Ladder

Porkins and Sally were riding their horses through the mountains.

The two of them had gone to Little Block to buy the horses, but when they got there the villagers had recognized them from the battle in the Nether and given them the horses for free.

They'd ridden down the road to Villagertropolis, but as they'd got closer they had spotted some robot guards up ahead.

"Which way now?" Porkins had asked. "Will we have to go over the mountains?"

"No," Sally had replied. "I know another road, an old road. Hopefully the robots won't know about it."

Sally's "road" was a tiny track that wound its way through the mountains. It was an ancient road, according to Sally. The Old People has used it, many years ago, but now it had been neglected and left to ruin.

It was quicker than climbing across the mountains though, and Porkins and Sally had made good time. Before long they'd come out the other side of the mountains, and could see Villagertropolis.

Even though it was nearby, Sally had never seen Villagertropolis before, and had been amazed at how big it was.

So now Porkins and Sally were riding their horses through the fields towards the city walls.

"How are we going to get inside?" Sally asked Porkins. "It looks like the gates are shut."

"We'll find a quiet bit, one with no guards, and we'll build a ladder," said Porkins.

"Will you be alright climbing a ladder?" Sally asked. "You know, with your... arm."

Porkins hadn't even thought of that. He kept forgetting that he was now one arm short, but then he'd try and pull on the horse's reign or scratch his nose and he'd be reminded all over again.

This will take some getting used to, he thought sadly.

After passing several farmhouses and riding through fields of animals and fields of crops, they finally reached the city wall and climbed off of their horses.

Porkins put down a crafting table and pulled out some wood from his backpack.

"A ladder... a ladder," he muttered to himself. "It's

been so long since I've made one that I've jolly well forgotten the recipe."

"Three sticks on either side and one in the middle row," said Sally.

"Ah yes, thank you!" said Porkins excitedly. He put a wood block down on the table, turning it into planks, then he put two planks blocks on the table, one on top of the other, and they turned to sticks. Then he placed the sticks down as Sally had suggested—three in the left column, one in the middle and three in the right column—and some ladders appeared.

"What-ho!" said Porkins. "Right, let's take a look inside the city, shall we?"

He placed a ladder block against the stone wall.

Immediately an alarm went off, blue lights flashing on the top of the wall.

"*INTRUDER ALERT!*" a robotic voice declared from some speakers on the wall. "*INTRUDER ALERT!*"

"Oh crumbs," said Porkins.

CHAPTER NINETEEN

The Robot King

"You're not Robo-Steve," said Carl. "Robo-Steve is all metal-looking. You're all gold-looking."

"When we last met my outer shell was badly damaged," said Robo-Steve. "So I decided to build myself a new body. From my research I have discovered that throughout history the colors gold and purple have often been associated with royalty, so when I declared myself king, I changed my outer casing to gold and changed the color of my eye bulbs to purple."

"You seem different," said Dave. "Last time we saw you, you said you'd changed. The electricity from the gas on Cool Island... did it do something to your brain?"

"That's correct," said Robo-Steve. "In my short life I have experienced many changes in my directives and personality. Recently I have been facing what you would call a personality crisis. I have been questioning who I am and what I want."

"So you've decided you want to put a crown on your

head and take over the world," said Carl. "Very original."

"It was not a decision I came to easily," said Robo-Steve. "But after much thought, I decided that this is the most logical course of action."

"How can taking over the world be logical?" said Dave.

"I will explain," said Robo-Steve. "But first let me show you something."

He stood up and walked over to a door. Dave and Carl were forced to follow by the blue robot guards surrounding them.

"One thing first," said Robo-Steve, turning round, "even though we've met twice, I'm afraid I don't know your names."

"Dave," said Dave.

"Carl," said Carl.

"Thank you," said Robo-Steve.

Dave couldn't get over how different Robo-Steve was. The first time he'd met him, back in Snow Town, Robo-Steve had been a mindless machine who just did whatever Ripley, his creator, commanded. On Cool Island Robo-Steve had been a warrior without mercy, fighting for his life. But now he was polite and softly spoken. The difference was remarkable.

Robo-Steve led them into a huge room. It had obviously been used for important things in the past—the walls were covered in wood panels, there were fancy paintings on the walls and there was a huge fireplace—but now it was full of animals in pens.

He brought them over to a pen full of cows.

"Robot cows," said Robo-Steve. "They look just like the real thing."

He was right, thought Dave. If he hadn't been told they were robots, he would have had no idea. The cows were even eating grass—the floor inside their pen had been dug up and replaced with grass blocks.

"Well if they're just like real cows, what's the point?" asked Carl.

"They're seventy-five percent more efficient than normal cows," said Robo-Steve. "They produce milk at a faster rate than normal cows, and they produce more milk per amount of grass eaten. They're better than normal cows in every way."

Robo-Steve opened the fence, walked into the pen, then milked one of the cows over a bucket. When the bucket was full, he held it down to Carl.

"Here," said Robo-Steve. "Taste it."

"Um, no thanks," said Carl.

"I insist," said Robo-Steve. "You'll enjoy it, I promise."

Carl leaned forward and took a sip of milk.

"Hmm, doesn't taste too bad," he said. "I'd better take another sip, just to make sure.

He took another sip.

"Not bad," he said, licking his lips. "I guess I'll try another sip."

He took another, then another, then grabbed the bucket in his mouth and poured it all down his throat.

"WOW!" said Carl, milk all over his face.

"Did you like it?" Robo-Steve asked.

"I guess it was alright," muttered Carl. "Got any more?"

Robo-Steve got Carl another bucket of milk, then showed them around the room. According to Robo-Steve his robot horses were faster than regular horses, his robot sheep produced more wool than regular sheep and his robot wolves were twice as powerful and ten times more loyal than regular wolves.

"With robotics I can make improved versions of every mob," said Robo-Steve. "I'm even thinking of creating some robot ocelots."

"No!" said Carl. "I mean, er, no... that's not a good idea."

"Robot animals are one thing," said Dave. "But you've turned all the villagers into slaves."

"They're not slaves," said Robo-Steve, "they've just had the logical sections of their brains enhanced. I've made them *better*. They're more productive, more intelligent and their sadness levels keep going down. Villagertropolis is a much better city now than before I arrived, and soon I'll start improving the rest of the world."

Robo-Steve pressed a button on the back of his hand and one of his fingertips opened up, revealing a tiny microphone.

"Assemble the army in the plaza," he said into the microphone.

"Look," said Dave, "this is going to sound weird, but we... we met someone from the future."

"A time traveler?" said Robo-Steve. "How interesting. My research has shown me that most scientists believe time travel is impossible, so I would very much like to speak to this person."

"Well you can't," said Dave, "because he's... he's dead. But he came back from the future to warn us about you. This invasion you're about to start will cause twenty years of war. Many people will suffer. This perfect world you want to create, it's not going to happen."

Robo-Steve thought for a moment.

"That does not compute," he said. "I've run the calculations in my head thousands of times. Within a year, the whole world will be under my control, and every villager will wear a neuro-helmet."

"Look," said Dave, "I've learned that things rarely work out the way you plan. Look at the villager who created you, Ripley. He was a smart guy, but his plan to frame Steve went wrong. Ripley ended up dead and his village got destroyed."

"My father was indeed smart," said Robo-Steve, "although he didn't have the advantage of having a robot brain, like I do."

It felt weird to Dave to hear Robo-Steve call Ripley *father*, but he guessed it was true: Ripley had created Robo-Steve, so he was, in some sense, his dad.

Robo-Steve brought them to a small room full of sofas with a roaring fireplace.

"Sit," he told them. Dave and Carl sat. Four of the blue robot guards came in and stood in the corners of the room.

"This palace was where the mayor lived," said Robo-Steve. "After scanning her brain I found she was quite unsuited to being a mayor, so I've sent her to work in a bakery instead. Her brain function is perfectly suited for the skills needed to be a baker."

Robo-Steve sat down in an armchair.

"I was brought to Villagertropolis by a kind captain and his crew," said Robo-Steve, looking into the fire. "I was badly injured after our fight in the arena, and I wanted to get off of Cool Island."

Dave felt a pang of guilt. He, Carl and Porkins had left Robo-Steve in the arena, teleporting out as the electric gas had crept towards them, leaving the robot to his fate.

"As grateful as I was to the captain," continued Robo-Steve, "I couldn't help but notice how inefficient his crew were. The way they sailed the ship needed much improvement, in my opinion.

"Then when we arrived at Villagertropolis, the city was under attack by zombie pigmen. The villagers and their iron golems were doing a terrible job at fighting the pigmen, and instantly I could see hundreds of ways that they could be more efficient at fighting.

"I went to a factory near the docks and using my superior IQ I started assembling troops of my own, using whatever materials I could find. They were inferior to the robots I have now, but they did the job. My small army managed to defeat the much larger pigman army. The pigmen retreated back to the Nether.

"The villagers were overjoyed. It was a new experience for me, to have people look at me with admiration, rather than fear. I wanted to do something to help them. To improve their lives. So I invented the neuro-helmet. It would allow every one of them to maximize their productivity. As well as making them more logical, it would scan their brain and find out what they were best at, making sure that everyone did the job that they were most suited to.

"The people of Villagertropolis trusted me so much that they eagerly accepted the helmets. Overnight the city was transformed—the people were more productive and less unhappy. A few villagers resisted the helmets, but I made my robots force them to put one on. I knew it was for their own good.

"In a matter of hours my robots had rebuilt the damage the pigmen had done to the city. I closed the city gates, in case another attack came, and concentrated on making Villagertropolis the most efficient city in history. We would produce exactly the right amount of food, none of it going to waste, and everyone would have a job which best suited their talents. It was a paradise."

"Your idea of paradise sounds a lot different than mine," muttered Carl.

"However, I knew this perfect system couldn't last," continued Robo-Steve. "I knew that one day others would come. Maybe villagers from other settlements would feel that the villagers of Villagertropolis were being controlled, and would try to free them. I decided that the only logical course of action was to take over the world, turning every village, town and city into a paradise of logic and reason. There will be no more struggle, no more war, no-one going hungry. It will be an end to suffering."

"But there'll be no more fun, no love, no emotions," said Dave. "You're turning everyone into mindless robots!"

"From what I have seen of emotions, they only lead to illogical decisions," said Robo-Steve.

Suddenly the door burst open and a robot came in. Like the others,this one looked like Steve, but he was made of red metal instead of blue.

"Your majesty," said the robot, "we have caught two more intruders. We found them trying to build a ladder over the wall. I don't think they're very intelligent, if I'm being honest."

"Thank you, Charles," said Robo-Steve. "Bring then in."

"Bring in the idiots," said the red robot, Charles.

One of the blue robots pushed two prisoners into the room.

"Porkins!" said Dave. "Sally!"

"Hello, Dave old chap," said Porkins sadly. "I'm afraid I'm in a jolly pickle again. I came to save you and Carl and... well, I didn't do a very good job of it."

"No you didn't," said Carl. "Although we got captured too, so I guess we can't talk."

"Of course you got captured, idiot," said the red robot with a sneer. "None of you have the intelligence of a robot. Your brains are so inferior to ours that you never stood a chance."

"That's enough, Charles," said Robo-Steve. "Please show our four guests to the balcony. The troops should all have gathered in the plaza by now."

"Look," said Carl, "you've won. Well done. Now why don't you just put those stupid helmets on us and get it over with? I don't know if I can stand much more of your talking."

"You will all receive neuro-helmets in time," said Robo-Steve, "but first I want to prove to you that my logical methods of ruling work. I don't want to force you to wear a neuro-helmet if you don't want you. I'm hoping that, in time, you'll see that my way is right, and that you'll actually *ask* to wear a helmet."

"I can't see that happening," said Carl.

"Well, we'll see," said Robo-Steve. "Now please, let's go to the balcony. It's time for my invasion to begin."

CHAPTER TWENTY

The Robot Army

Robo-Steve and his robot guards led them onto a balcony that overlooked the plaza below. When Dave saw the plaza, it made him gasp.

Hundreds—maybe *thousands*—of blue robots had gathered together, all stood in perfectly neat rows. And they weren't just gathered in the plaza, they were lined up in the streets too. The city was full of them.

There's so many of them, Dave thought in disbelief. He'd thought Herobrine's zombie pigman army had been big, but that was nothing compared to this.

Villagers in neuro-helmets were looking out of every window and balcony at the robots. They all had bored expressions on their faces.

"Today is a great day, my soldiers," Robo-Steve shouted down at the robots. "Today we spread logic and reason throughout the world. You will march from village to town, ensuring every villager has a neuro-helmet of their own. A new, better worlds begins today.

"EIYYEEEEEEEEEEEE!!!!"

A terrible scream echoed across the city.

"What the blazes was that?" said Porkins.

But Dave knew what it was.

"Uh oh," said Carl.

BOOOM!!!

From far across the city, Dave saw a portion of the city wall get blown to bits by a blast of blue fire.

"What is that?" said Robo-Steve. "Charles, go and find out what that is."

But they didn't have to wait to find out. A huge blue creature was charging down one of the wide streets that led to the plaza, sending robots flying as it crashed into them.

"It's coming this way!" said Charles, the red robot. "Your majesty, we must evacuate!"

The creature burst into the plaza, trampling robots as it came to a stop. The remaining robots just stood still, still standing to attention as if nothing had happened.

As Dave had suspected, it was the blue creeper queen. But what he had *not* expected was to see a villager riding on the creeper queen's back.

"It's Future Dave!" gasped Carl. "He's alive!"

Future Dave has tied some rope around the queen's neck, using it as reigns like one would on a horse. He had his bow and arrow aimed at the balcony; the arrow glowing red.

"Get away from the Robot King," he yelled to Dave and the others. "He must be destroyed!"

CHAPTER TWENTY-ONE

Changing the Future

Future Dave let go of the exploding arrow, and it sped through the air towards the balcony.

Carl, Porkins and Sally all jumped out of the way. Robo-Steve just stood in place, too surprised to move. Without thinking, Dave pushed Robo-Steve out of the path of the arrow. The arrow whizzed past them, through the balcony doors, through the big room with the animals then into the room with the sofas, blowing it to bits.

Robo-Steve lay on the floor, looking up at Dave with confusion.

"Why did you save me?" he asked. "If your goal is to stop my invasion, that was a most illogical decision."

"I saved you because... because I don't think you're really a bad guy," said Dave. "I just think you're a bit confused."

"Incorrect," said Robo-Steve. "My programming makes it impossible for me to be confused."

"Really?" said Dave. "Because to me you look

confused. You were programmed to be a mindless machine who obeyed every word of your creator, then you went against your creator, then you begged us to save you at the Cool Dude Battle Royale, and now you're planning to take over the world. It seems to me that you *are* confused: you don't know what you want, or what you want to do with your life, and that's fine."

Dave turned to look at his friends.

"Carl was a moody creeper whose only goal in life was to blow himself up," said Dave. "Now he's a slightly-less moody creeper who's joined me on my stupid quest to find a dragon. Also, he used to hate fighting, and now he loves it."

He turned to Porkins.

"Porkins has had to adapt to leaving his home and losing everyone he ever loved," said Dave. "He lost his family, but he found a new one with me and Carl."

"I see him as a sort-of annoying younger brother," said Carl. "The kind of one who wets the bed and always steals your toys."

"You don't have to be who you were programmed to be," said Dave to Robo-Steve. "Look at me—I'm a villager. I'm not supposed to do anything but trade and farm, but I've chosen to try and become a hero."

Robo-Steve thought for a moment.

"You make some interesting points, Dave," he said.

"Perhaps a purely logical outlook has given me a limited view of the world. Maybe it would be best if I broaden my horizons, and see what the world has to offer before deciding to conquer it."

"NO!"

It was Future Dave. He had a glowing red arrow strung on his bow, aiming right at Robo-Steve.

"You don't get to start again, not after what you've done," Future Dave said to Robo-Steve. "I've lost too many good people to let you off the hook!"

Dave stepped in front of Robo-Steve, protecting him from Future Dave.

"Out of my way!" shouted Future Dave.

"No," said Dave. "He can change, I know he can."

"If he's going to change, then why am I still here?" said Future Dave. "If the war isn't going to happen, then I would never be sent back in time. So the fact that I'm still here means that the war *does* happen. The Robot King is going to destroy everything you've ever loved. I know because I've watched it happen to me."

Robo-Steve got to his feet.

"I assume this is the time traveler that you mentioned earlier," he said to Dave. "He makes a valid point. If I am going to change my ways and stop my invasion, as you hope, why would he not be erased from this timeline?"

"I... I don't know," said Dave.

"Perhaps it would be best if you let him destroy me," said Robo-Steve. "If I'm going to cause so much pain, it may be best."

"No," said Dave. "I... I can't."

"Listen to me, you stupid robot," said Sally. Dave was surprised to see that she was crying.

"I have to believe that bad people can change," Sally continued. "My husband did... he did some terrible things. But I still love him, and I need to believe that he can turn good again. If anyone can help you change your ways, it's Dave. He turned my village of farmers into warriors in a matter of days. If you went along with him, and joined him on his quest, who knows how much you'd change."

"Wait, what?" said Carl. "No way is this crazy robot joining us!"

"That sounds like a spiffing idea," said Porkins. "It'll be lovely to have another companion on the road."

Carl rolled his eyes. "Porkins you loony," he said.

Robo-Steve turned to Dave.

"Your female friend makes a valid point," he said, looking at Sally. "I know your feelings towards me are probably extremely negative, but, if you'll have me, I would like to join you on your travels. Perhaps along the way I will learn to look at the world in a different way."

Dave grinned. "Of course," he said. "Of course you're welcome to join us."

"Oh great," said Carl, "another weirdo."

Robo-Steve stepped forward, looking over the balcony at his robot army.

"What are you doing?" Future Dave said. "If you try anything..."

"Emergency code five one seven nine two," Robo-Steve said, his voice booming loudly across the city. "Initiate self destruct."

"AFFIRMATIVE!" all the robots said together. Then *BOOM BOOM BOOM BOOM BOOM* they all started to explode. Within a few seconds they were all destroyed, leaving nothing but bits of blue metal on the ground.

"Wow," said Carl.

The only robot left was Charles.

"W-What are you doing, your majesty?" he asked.

"Emergency code three three two," said Robo-Steve. "Deactivate all neuro-helmets."

This was less spectacular. Instead of lots of explosions, the red lights on the helmets of the villagers all began to turn off, and the villagers started removing their helmets, looking around like they were waking from a dream.

Suddenly, for the first time since Dave had arrived there, the city was full of people talking. It was like a completely different city.

"What... what's happening to me?"

It was Future Dave. He was starting to disappear.

"It's working!" he said happily. "You changed the future! Thank you, all of y—"

And then he was gone.

CHAPTER TWENTY-TWO

A New Companion

After a lot of debate, the villagers of Villagertropolis decided to let Robo-Steve go free.

"He did save us from the pigmen," said the mayor, a stern-looking woman in a sharp suit. "But if he tries anything like this again, he's gonna be in big trouble."

"Thank you Mrs Mayor," said Robo-Steve. "And I apologize once again for the trouble my actions have caused."

She also let Charles stay on in the city, keeping him on as her assistant.

The other question was, what were they going to do with the giant blue creeper queen? Future Dave seemed to have tamed it, and as it walked around the city plaza it didn't seem to be hurting anyone, but they all agreed that it couldn't stay.

"If it explodes it'll destroy the whole city!" said the mayor.

"You know, Dave old chap," said Porkins, "since the

blighter was tamed by future-you, maybe it'll obey present-you as well?"

So as much as it terrified him, Dave had to climb onto the creeper queen's back, grab onto her reins and ride her carefully out of the city; Carl, Porkins, Robo-Steve and Sally following at a safe distance behind.

Dave brought the creeper queen to the foot of the mountains, then climbed off.

"Um, you're free now," he told her. "Off you go."

"*SKIIIIIE!!!*" the creeper queen said, leaning down and nuzzling her blue face against Dave.

"I think she likes you," grinned Carl.

"I think I've never been so terrified," said Dave.

Next, Dave, Carl, Porkins, Robo-Steve and Sally made their way back to Greenleaf. They didn't have horses, but the main road was clear of robots now, so it was much easier going than crossing the mountains or going along the old road.

When they reached the village, a couple of days later, Dave asked Sally if she wanted to join them on their journey.

"Thank you, but no," she said, smiling. "I know it's silly, but I want to stay here. In case Adam comes home."

So they said their goodbyes, then Dave, Porkins, Carl and their new companion, Robo-Steve, went on their way.

"What is our destination?" asked Robo-Steve. "How

do you know which direction to go to get to this ender dragon?"

"Well," said Dave, "first let's go to Little Block and get some horses, and then I'll show you."

"Affirmative," said Robo-Steve.

"*Affirmative*," said Carl, rolling his eyes. "I never thought I'd say this, Porkins, but you're no longer the biggest idiot in our group."

"Thanks very much," said Porkins, smiling.

Carl just shook his head.

"Oh how I wish I could just blow myself up," he said. "If only for a bit of peace and quiet."

EPILOGUE

It had been a long week on the road and Porkins was feeling worn out. Not only had it been raining all week, but his remaining arm was aching. It was no easy thing to control a horse with one hand, and he was really feeling the strain.

Porkins could hear Dave and Carl snoring in their beds, but as tired as he was, he just couldn't get to sleep. He got up and went outside.

Robo-Steve was leaning against the wall of the house, looking up at the stars.

"It's strange," said Robo-Steve. "Even though I have an IQ of over 3,000, I have no idea what stars are. I have theories, of course, but even with all my knowledge I don't know everything. I don't how the world began. I don't know where life came from. There are so many mysteries that logic alone can't solve."

"I guess that's true," said Porkins. "Sometimes it's hard to know what the answer to even the simplest question is. I'm still not sure if I've made the right decision staying with Dave and Carl, or whether I should have joined my people in Little Bacon. It's a real pickle."

"I have noticed you've been struggling mentally," said Robo-Steve. "I'm beginning to become more attuned to emotions. I've also noticed that you've been operating at less than one-hundred percent thanks to your missing arm."

"Yes, it has been difficult," said Porkins, clutching the bare skin where his arm had once been. "But I guess it's just something I'll have to jolly well get used to."

"Perhaps not," said Robo-Steve. "I made you this."

He handed Porkins a strange metal object. For a moment Porkins had no clue what it was, and then he realized: it was a robot arm!

"I'm eighty-nine per cent sure it will work," said Robo-Steve. "Just place it on your shoulder, and it should attach magnetically.

Porkins took the robot arm and pushed it against his shoulder. Amazingly, it did seem to stick, as if by magic. For a moment the arm hung limp, like it was just a bit of metal attached to his body, but then Porkins could *feel* it. He tried to move the arm, and found out that he could.

"Good gravy!" said Porkins.

"It may take some getting used to," said Robo-Steve. "I estimate between three and five weeks."

Porkins leaped forward and gave Robo-Steve a hug. His body was cold and hard, but Porkins didn't mind.

"This is an unusual show of gratitude," said Robo-Steve. "What is it called?"

"A hug," said Porkins, grinning.

"A hug..." said Robo-Steve. "An interesting word. I will add it to my data banks."

*

Dave wiped the sleep from his eyes. The morning light was coming through the windows, and Carl and Porkins's beds were empty. He went outside. Carl was sitting against the wall of the house, watching Porkins and Robo-Steve practice sword fighting in the distance.

It took Dave a moment to realize what was so odd about this scene. But then it came to him.

"Porkins... has two arms!" he said to Carl.

"Yeah, apparently Robo-Steve built him a new one," said Carl. "Maybe that robot isn't so bad after all."

"Yeah," said Dave, grinning. "Maybe not."

"Listen," said Carl, "I know you like to believe that everyone can change, that we should give everyone a second chance, and that's fine. I'm big enough to admit I was wrong about Robo-Steve. But you need to realize that when it comes to Herobrine, it's not gonna work like that."

Dave felt a familiar cold tingle down his spine as Carl said the word *Herobrine.*

"I know that," said Dave.

"I hope so," said Carl. "Because you're not going to be able to say nice words to Herobrine to make him see the error of his ways. He's not going to become your new best friend and join you on your quest."

Dave watched Robo-Steve and Porkins play-fighting with their swords. Yes, Robo-Steve had changed his ways, but Carl was right—Herobrine *was* different. He wasn't misguided like Robo-Steve, bitter like Ripley, cowardly like Adam or stupid like Derek Cool. Of all the villains they'd met on their travels, Herobrine was the only one Dave would call *evil.*

"Don't worry," Dave said to Carl. "If we do ever meet Herobrine again, and it comes down to it, I'll do the right thing..."

TO BE CONTINUED...